WHAT IS IN THE BACKGROUND? BYSTANDER'S PERSPECTIVE

I feel so
uncomfortable
Why did we come back here after everything with time travellers and Blue Mouse channel all kicking off last time we came here!
*Giggles
*Giggles

Victor......I've told you....you were
dreaming.....we're not gonna hear any more talk
about time travel are we?

This is exactly what happened last time
Okay. So we are talking about this then?
It's true! Last time I was on this cruise ship it all started with this random man turning invisible
I remember...I am confident I didn't imagine it, him and his friend, they just vanished

2015

SCOFFS
Whispers Who talks like that?
GASP Something is coming our way! We have to hide for the sake of my programme!
Time to use my expertise

Him and his assistant quickly turned invisible, ZAP! The couple drinking in the background were very shocked but assumed it was the alcohol
ZOP!

In a secret cabin one agent was looking at the live feed of the time machine of her tablet while several looked at a screen and one guy was acting like a fool with a doofy mask

They all immediately started betraying each other
Sue with that stuff I planted in your cabin it's pretty obvious you were the mastermind behind all of this. "But officers if I didn't listen to her, I was scared she could have done it to me!"
Every man for himself!
There's no evidence against me, I'm afraid you're the only criminal here
Unfortunately for you I have recorded everything you just said

1 minute earlier this black ball had appeared in the ocean (Which was now heading towards the boat) Also an invisible Blue Mouse grunt had radioed in

Then suddenly
WOO

Darren: The clone of that Serena over there must have come from her D.N.A but for some reason there is no record of it in the A.C.L files
Ben: How do the time force know that?
Darren: Because the time force hacked into their files
Darren: May theorized that the Serena Clone comes from another universe
Cary: Hey Darren isn't that the cruise ship from Larry's comics, the Dronoser comic that was like "When the beings of the mind extend to reality" and the Blue Mouse one too!
Ben: Larry, the one you mentioned at the bar
Darren: Yes, Larry made comics and made them all come to this universe in 2020, fortunately I was able to go back in time and freeze him and obtain several copies of his comics in order to know more about them, for example I knew that the cruise ship over there is full of invisible fees and our past selves are about to land in the water right over there

Victor saw in one of the cabins windows that faries were in there!

The fairies stood on the computer desk and started enchanting the masks, the blue mouse channel grunts needed them but the enchantment was now set

One person by the pool said
Can't believe I actually married this guy
I went to the bar but everyone had gone, hope they don't all become missing people cases hahahahahaha! Well, that wasn't very funny

Then Victor saw a man jump off the ship in front of his wife then felt some invisible person run passed him!!! Victor ran to tell Yvonne!
RED ALERT! RED ALERT!
Oh come on I wasn't that bad of a wife!

Victor had seen the whole thing!
W-what!? H-he just disappeared!!!!
And in there is fairies and AND! oh where is Yvonne!

Yvonne was talking to a guy
Hahahah ahaha
Hahahahaha So, you know like, there's a great bar down the deck if you wanna-

Yvonne! Yvonne! A MEMBER OF STAFF JUST TURNED INVISIBLE RIGHT IN FRONT OF ME!?
THEN SOME GUY JUMPED OFF THE BOAT TO GET AWAY FORM HIS WIFE THEN THERE WAS FARIES THEN

Victor sweetie, that's um, that's, *Whispers* have you taken your meds?

No I haven't, I'll go look for them now

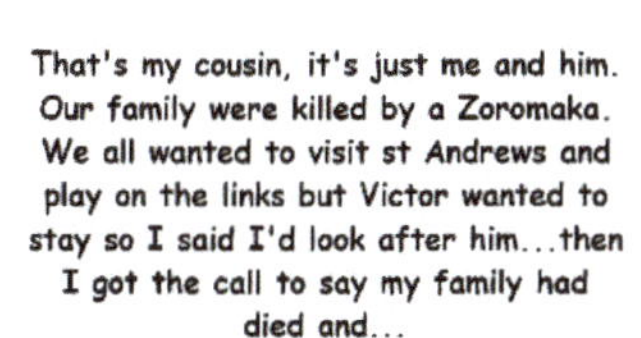

That's my cousin, it's just me and him. Our family were killed by a Zoromaka. We all wanted to visit st Andrews and play on the links but Victor wanted to stay so I said I'd look after him...then I got the call to say my family had died and...
W-what?

The man suddenly shot off!
NO! THANK! YOU!
DASH!

She never listens to me!

Suddenly a big massive round ball appeared right in front of him!!!!
(People could be heard talking inside!!!!!)

I-I-
iit's
it's I-
I-it's
not real
It's
..........P-proof

Present Day
But then when I get to the time machine with Yvonne it's just vanished?
Then all of a sudden fairies are making people fly then I see time travellers and Blue Mouse employees fighting then I see the time travellers sleeping for eight hours then I see them fighting again then they vanish....

2015
I'm going to space! Thank you Faries!
WOW! It's just like magic!
This feels like a dream

Hey! Spiffy tech you got there. Invisible huh?

SPLOOSH

SPLOOSH

Everyone stay where you are!
TICK! TICK!

Dude. I just dry cleaned this suit!

Now that you know our secret tech, we can't let you live

AAAAAAAHHH HHHHHHH!!!!!!
I'm sending you the dry cleaning bill
AAAAAAAAHHHHHHHHHHH!!!!!!!!!!!!
Oh you're on
Let's dance

I have used this hour hand to waste time
You shall remain frozen in time for two hours

I have this red second hand of a clock to speed myself up and
And this hour hand from a clock to slow YOU down so don't try it (They should be grateful I don't have a minute hand on me)

Garrison behind you LOOK

What is it Caryl?

You can get a Nicky Mouse shaped waffle for only one dollar!
...pretty cool right?.....Darren? .....Why are you looking at me so angrily?

hee hee

SSSSS
Sweet dreams

THUD.
SSSSS!
THUD.
Have...to...stay awake...
Wait...but I....like....blue mouse....channel .....ZZZZZZZ

On Blue mouse employee was radioing in to another invisible employee that was on the side deck. They were letting him know that the fairies have all escaped and tampered with the masks and the blue mouse gas attack at the three intruders at the bar went through their masks and knocked them out too!? Burt they now are about to drag the unconscious time travellers to their cabin

A few seaconds earlier Ben suddenly woke up after the gas attack!

He made a run for it and was now heading towards the invisible blue mouse guy who was radioing in

POW! The invisible hand punched him in the face knocking Ben out clean

8 Hours later

GASP Where are we!?

GASP!
GASP!

It's okay here let me
fix your pillow

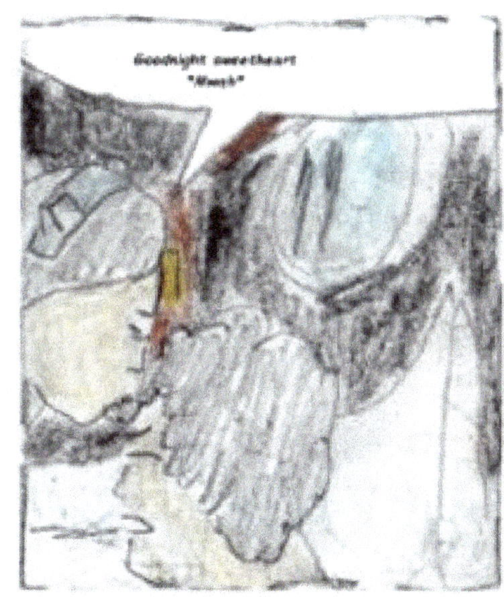
Goodnight sweetheart
"Mmph"

Would you like the
door open or
closed?

If you don't let me stay then I'm gonna tell dad!

This woman's husband works for blue mouse and he is not a great guy

GASP DON'T TELL HIM!

More opponents!? Who is this guy!?

Okay they're reeled in, this guy is working with Harry and is helping him defeat us and something to do with Serena Carpenter and her boyfriend, also everyone in the bar got thrown overboard but the fairies saved them with the pixie dust, oh yeah and the fairies have still escaped oh and apparently the three time travellers have escaped from their cabin, what the heck is my life.

So, we're good, WHO CARES ABOUT SOME GA... THIS GUY IS RUNNING ALL OVER THE PLACE KNOCKING OUT ALL OF US! Excuse me Blair but can you go back to your own universe please we have enough to deal with

Ben saw Blair knock out the goons and was impressed, but who was Blair, must be someone from another story

POW!

Ben: That....that is power, whoever that is, they are not from this world

Blue Mouse Channel were trying to get into the time machine!!!!?????
W-w-why do we have to stop them why not get a grown up to do it!?
Ben you're 26
I can't believe that woman just kissed my forehead like that
Darren rushed over in a split second with his second hand
WOOSH
He defeated all of them in a mili-seacond
SLASH
SLASH

Suddenly more Blue Mouse Channel grunts appeared!? They were invisible!
We really, really, really, really, really, really, really, really, really really don't want to fight you
Maybe we can come to some sort of agreement?
Guess not....

Cory:

I'm not going to be weird like Blue Mouse Channel anymore

Present Day
Oh you hadn't taken your medication that day
Sigh I didn't need to
Blue mouse channel were secretly watching
Yvonne how did I end up being stuck looking after you?
Yvonne: You looking AFTER ME! IS THAT A JOKE!
They were about to strike!
To be continued